How Camel Got Hump

and Other Stories

Contents

How the Camel Got His Hump

Retold from a
story by Rudyard Kipling

Long, long ago, there was
a camel. When anyone asked
him to work, he said "Humph!"
Just "Humph!" and no more.

One day, the horse came
to him and said, "Camel,
oh, Camel! Come and work
like the rest of us."

"Humph!" said the camel.

So the horse went away
and told the man.

3

Then the dog came
to the camel and said, "Camel,
oh, Camel! Come and work
like the rest of us."

"Humph!" said the camel.

So the dog went away
and told the man.

Soon the ox came to see the camel. He said, "Camel, oh, Camel! Come and work like the rest of us."

"Humph!" said the camel.

So the ox went away and told the man.

5

At the end of three days,
the man called the horse,
the dog, and the ox together.
"My animals, I am sorry,
but the camel won't work.
So you will have to work harder
to make up for him," he said.

The animals were angry.
They met to talk about what
should be done. It was decided
that the horse would go and talk
to the wise man of the desert.

"Is it right to be idle?"
the horse asked the wise man.
"No," said the wise man.
"Well," said the horse,
"the camel hasn't done any
work for the last three days."

8

"Have you asked him to work?"
said the wise man.

"Yes, but he just says 'Humph!'"
said the horse.

"Very well," said the wise man.
"I will talk to him."

9

Soon the wise man found
the lazy camel.

"My long-legged friend,"
said the wise man, "why don't
you work?"

"Humph!" said the camel.

The wise man sat down.
He began to think.

"You've given the horse, the dog, and the ox more work because you are idle," said the wise man.

"Humph!" said the camel.

"I would not say that again if I were you," said the wise man. "You might say it once too often. I want you to work!"

However, the naughty camel
said "Humph!" again.

No sooner had he said it
than his back began to twitch.
It started puffing up and up.
It puffed all the way up
into a great big lolloping humph.

"Now you have your very own humph," said the wise man. "Now you will work."

"How can I with this humph on my back?" said the camel.

"That humph will help you work," said the wise man.

"You missed three days of work, but now you can work for three days without eating, because you can live off the fat in your humph. So get to work now and behave!"

So the camel went – humph and all – to work with the horse, the dog, and the ox.

From that day to this, the camel has had a humph (we call it a "hump" now, so as not to hurt his feelings). But he has never caught up on the three days of work he missed long, long ago, and he has never yet learned to behave.

Why Elephants Have Long Noses

Retold from a
story by Rudyard Kipling

Long, long ago, all elephants had short noses.

Then, one day, a curious little elephant asked his mother, "What do crocodiles like to eat?"

"Crocodiles!" said his mother. "That's a terrible word. Never, never, never say that word!"

However, the little elephant was very curious. He wanted to know about crocodiles. He wanted to know what they liked to eat. So he went to look for crocodiles. He saw a crocodile in the river.

"Hello there, Crocodile," called
the little elephant. "Tell me,
what do you like to eat?"

19

"I can't hear you," called the crocodile. "Come a little closer."

So the little elephant went to the edge of the river.

"I said, 'What do you like to eat?'"

"Ah," said the crocodile. "That is a secret. Bend down and I will whisper it in your ear."

So the little elephant bent
down towards the crocodile.

The cunning crocodile
came very, very close and said,
"Crocodiles like to eat little
elephants!"

And he grabbed the little
elephant by the nose.

The little elephant pulled and pulled. The crocodile pulled and pulled. They pulled and pulled until, finally, the crocodile let go.

They had pulled so hard
that the little elephant's nose
had stretched.

And that is why, from that
day to this, elephants have had
long noses.

Why the Bear Has a Short Tail

Retold from
an old Norwegian tale

Long, long ago, Bear had
a long tail. Then, one day,
Bear met Fox. Fox was carrying
some fish that he had stolen.

"Where did you get those fish?"
asked Bear.

"Oh, I went fishing and caught
them," replied Fox.

"I'd like to learn to fish,"
said Bear.

"It's easy," said Fox. "Go out on the lake and cut a hole in the ice. Then sit down and stick your tail into the hole."

"Is that all?" asked Bear.

"No," said Fox. "You must sit there for a long, long while, and you must keep very still. The longer you keep your tail in the water, the more fish you will catch. Then, after a long, long time, stand up and jerk your tail out of the water."

So Bear did what Fox had said.
He cut a hole in the ice.
He held his tail in the ice hole
for a long, long time. His tail
stung, but Bear kept very still.

"I must have some fish by now," said Bear, and he stood up.

However, when he tried to pull out his tail, his tail was frozen. It snapped right off.

And, to this day, bears have had short tails.

FROM THE ILLUSTRATORS

Travelling in Egypt and India taught me a thing or two about camels... they bite, they smell, and their humps are very uncomfortable to ride on!

Jeffy James

I love to draw, cut, paint, and glue! One of my favourite subjects is animals, especially ones with big teeth, and chubby ones with very long noses!

Ellen Giggenbach

I work from my home at the beach. I like drawing bears, but I've never met one in the wild – thank goodness!

Martin Bailey